The Bremen-Town Musicians

Retold and illustrated by
Ilse Plume

Dragonfly Books 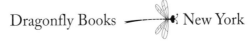 New York

All rights reserved. Published in the United States by Dragonfly Books,
an imprint of Random House Children's Books, a division of Random House, Inc., New York.
Originally published in hardcover in the United States
by Doubleday Books for Young Readers, Garden City, in 1980.

Dragonfly Books with the colophon is a registered trademark of Random House, Inc.

Visit us on the Web! www.randomhouse.com/kids

Educators and librarians, for a variety of teaching tools,
visit us at www.randomhouse.com/teachers

The Library of Congress has cataloged the hardcover edition of this work as follows:
Plume, Ilse.
The Bremen town musicians / retold and illustrated by Ilse Plume.
p. cm.
Summary: A retelling of the Grimm tale in which an old donkey, dog, cat, and rooster,
no longer wanted by their masters, set out for Bremen to become musicians.
ISBN 978-0-385-15161-0 (trade) — ISBN 978-0-440-41456-8 (pbk.)
[1. Fairy tales. 2. Folklore—Germany.] I. Title.
PZ8.P727 Br
398.2/452/0943 E
79006622

MANUFACTURED IN CHINA

18 17

FOR MY "GUARDIAN ANGEL"
PETER   AND FOR
MY MOTHER
ALICE.....
WITH
LOVE !!

A very long time ago there lived an old donkey who had served a miller faithfully for many years. But when the donkey had become too old to carry heavy sacks of grain on his back, his master was tempted to do away with him and save himself the expense of feeding such a useless beast.

Fearing the worst, the donkey took to the open road while he still had the use of his four legs. As he walked, he decided that since he had such a wonderful bray, he would go to Bremen-town and join a band of street musicians there.

The donkey had not gone far when he came upon an old hunting dog lying in the road and panting as if he had run a long way.

"Hey, old four-paws, what's the matter?" asked the donkey. "Why are you panting so hard?"

"Oh!" gasped the dog. "What is to become of me? Now that I am old and stiff and can't hunt anymore, my master plans to shoot me! I have run away, but now I will surely starve since I have nowhere to go."

"Why not join me?" asked the donkey. "I am bound for Bremen-town to be a musician there. I will bray and you can bark and together we'll make wonderful music."

The dog was glad to go, so the two joined forces and went on down the road.

Before long they came upon a cat shivering by the roadside. She looked as sad as a rainy day, and her elegant whiskers drooped almost to the ground.

"Hey, old whisker-face!" said the donkey. "What is the matter with you? Nothing can be as bad as all that!"

"Little do you know," moaned the cat. "I am getting too old and weak to chase mice. Now that my eyes are failing and my teeth are no longer sharp, my mistress plans to drown me! I have run this far, but where can I go now?"

"Come with us," said the donkey. "We are off to Bremen-town to be musicians. Your singing would be most welcome."

So the cat joined them and the three traveled on together.

Soon the friends came to a farmyard, and there on the gatepost was a ragged old rooster. He was crowing so loudly that they stopped in their tracks and looked at him in amazement.

"Hey, red-comb, stop your screeching!" said the donkey. "Why are you making such a racket?"

"This is my last chance to crow, so I'm making all the noise I can," said the rooster. "Now that I'm not as young as I used to be, my mistress has decided to make me into chicken soup!"

"Listen," said the donkey, "come with us to Bremen-town and we can all be musicians there. You have a fine lusty crow, and no one would hear it in a kettle of soup!"

So the rooster gladly went along and the four runaways went on their way.

The friends walked on and on, but Bremen-town was still a long way off, and it was impossible to reach it in just one day. Toward nightfall the travelers stopped in the middle of a great, dark forest and decided to spend the night there.

Tired from the journey, the donkey and the dog lay down under a large tree, the cat settled herself on a low branch, and the rooster perched near the top to get a better view. From there he could see for miles, and as he looked around, he suddenly saw a bright light glittering through the trees.

Eagerly the rooster called down to his companions, "I see a light. There must be a house nearby!"

"Then let's go there at once," said the donkey. "This is not such a comfortable place to spend the night."

All the animals agreed. The dog had hopes of finding a few bones, and the cat longed for a saucer of milk.

At last they found themselves in front of the house, and the donkey crept up to the window to look in. Inside he saw a table heaped with good things to eat, and a band of robbers enjoying their feast.

"Hey, long-ears, what do you see?" the rooster asked. The donkey explained, and the four friends quickly thought of a way to get rid of the robbers.

The donkey stood with his front hooves on the windowsill, the dog jumped on the donkey's back, the cat climbed up on the dog, and the rooster perched on the cat.

At the donkey's signal they all made their music as loudly as they could. The donkey brayed, the dog barked, the cat meowed, and the rooster crowed. In the midst of this glorious uproar all four went plunging through the window into the robbers' den!

The robbers jumped up in fright, thinking that a pack of demons had attacked them, and ran screaming into the forest, fearing for their lives.

The four musicians rejoiced at their good luck in frightening the robbers away. They made themselves right at home and feasted as though they had not eaten in months. When they had finished their meal, they blew out the lantern and found a place for the night, each according to his own idea of comfort.

The donkey went outdoors and lay down in some straw. The dog stretched himself out behind the door. The cat curled up by the hearth. And the rooster flew up on the roof. Exhausted from their adventure, they quickly fell asleep.

After midnight had passed, the robbers came out of their hiding place. When they saw the house all dark and quiet, they thought they had been scared away too easily. The robber chief ordered one of his men to go back and look around.

Cautiously the man crept back through the night and went inside to light a candle at the hearth. There he saw the cat's eyes glowing in the dark and thought they were smoldering embers. But when he tried to light a match by them, the cat flew at him in a fury and scratched him as hard as she could! Before the robber could even reach the door, the dog jumped up and bit his leg, and as he ran across the yard, the donkey gave him a sharp kick. Hearing all the commotion, the rooster gave forth a piercing shriek, "Cock-a-doodle-doo! Cock-a-doodle-doo!"

The frightened robber did not stop running until he had reached the robber chief! Puffing and panting, he gasped, "In the house sits a fiendish witch, who snarled and scratched my face. By the door waits a bandit, who stabbed me in the leg with a knife. In the barnyard lurks a hairy monster, who attacked me with a club. But, worst of all, up on the roof crouches an old judge, who yelled, 'Catch the crook, do! Catch the crook, do!' We must never go back there again." And indeed they didn't.

As for our brave musicians, they didn't go to Bremen-town after all. They decided it would be a shame to leave such a comfortable house, and no doubt they are still there today, making wonderful music under the stars.